GET THE GIGGLES WITH

YUCK!

by Matt and Dave

Join Yuck's fanclub at
YUCKWEB.COM

**FOR FANTASTIC
FOOTBALLERS:**

Reece   You   Tilly

Daniel   Thomas

Pegin   Dylan   Ratty

Mark   Kieran

SIMON AND SCHUSTER

First published in Great Britain in 2010
by Simon & Schuster UK Ltd
A CBS COMPANY
1st Floor, 222 Gray's Inn Road, London WC1X 8HB

Text © Matthew Morgan and David Sinden 2010
Cover and inside illustrations © Nigel Baines 2010
This book is copyright under the Berne Convention.
No reproduction without permission.

The right of Matthew Morgan and David Sinden to be identified as
the authors of this work has been asserted by them in accordance with
sections 77 and 78 of the Copyright, Designs and Patents Act, 1988.

1 3 5 7 9 10 8 6 4 2

A CIP catalogue record for this book is
available from the British Library

ISBN 978-1-84738-747-9

Printed and bound in Great Britain by
Cox & Wyman Ltd Reading Berkshire

www.simonandschuster.co.uk
www.yuckweb.com

GET THE GIGGLES WITH

YUCK

by Matt and Dave

YUCK'S FANTASTIC FOOTBALL MATCH

AND

YUCK'S CREEPY CRAWLIES

Illustrated by Nigel Baines

YUCK'S FANTASTIC FOOTBALL MATCH

Yuck and his friends were playing football in the park. Yuck dribbled the ball around a dog poo then passed it to Little Eric who volleyed it to Schoolie Julie who back-heeled it to Tom Bum who chipped it to Fartin Martin who scissor-kicked it to Tall Paul who headed it to Clip-Clop Chloe who chipped it to Ben Bong who booted it to Kate the Skate who crossed it to Megan the Mouth who ran towards goal...

Frank the Tank was in goal. "No one scores past me!" he said waving his arms.

Megan the Mouth hesitated, unsure which way he'd dive.

Yuck raced up the pitch. "Over here, Megan!" he called.

Megan the Mouth passed the ball to Yuck, and he did a POWER STRIKE, blasting it as hard as he could. As he shot, a cloud of stinky cheesy gas puffed from his football boot.

"Phwoargh!" Frank the Tank said, smelling the pong. He covered his nose with his hands, and the ball shot straight past him blasting right through the net.

"Goal!" everyone cheered.

"Nice shot, Yuck," Little Eric said. "If we play as good as this next weekend, we'll definitely win the cup."

They were practising for next weekend's Cup Final between Yuck's All Stars and Hooray United. It was to be the biggest match of the year and Yuck was the All Star's star player and captain.

Frank the Tank wafted his hands to clear the stinky air. "Hooray United don't stand a chance against your stinky boots, Yuck!"

Yuck smiled. His football boots were mouldy and muddy and stank of toe cheese – and that's just how he liked them. They were his lucky boots and had scored the winning goal in every game this season.

Yuck saw the football rolling across the park from his POWER STRIKE. His sister, Polly Princess, and her friend, Juicy Lucy, were playing on the swings. He saw Polly dash to the ball and pick it up.

"Can we have it back, please?" Yuck called, running over.

Polly threw the ball into the duck pond. "Oops, I seem to have dropped it," she said.

"Hey, that's our team ball!" Yuck told her.

While Little Eric and Schoolie Julie ran to the pond to retrieve the ball, Yuck stood nose-to-nose with Polly. "There was no need for that," he said to her.

"You and your silly football team are just a bunch of losers," Polly sneered.

Little Eric and Schoolie Julie rushed over with the ball. They were wet and covered in pondweed.

"Did you have to do that, Polly?" Schoolie Julie asked. "We're trying to practise."

Polly eyed Schoolie Julie from head to toe and sniggered. "Practising to be swamp monsters by the looks of it."

"Actually, we're practising for the Cup Final," Little Eric said proudly. "We're going to win the trophy."

Polly's eyes widened. "What trophy?" she asked.

"The Cup Final trophy," Yuck told her. "The biggest trophy of all."

Yuck turned his back on Polly and walked away with Little Eric and Schoolie Julie.

Polly ran after them. "Yuck, please can I play in the Cup Final too?" she asked.

"Thanks, Polly, but we've already got enough players," Yuck replied.

"I could play instead of Schoolie Julie," Polly said, pushing Schoolie Julie to the ground.

Schoolie Julie got to her feet and wiped the mud from her knees. "I'm not giving my place to a bully," she said to Polly.

"Yeah, Polly, find your own team to play with," Little Eric added.

Polly stomped off across the park, and Juicy Lucy ran from the swings to join her.

"How come you want to play in the Cup Final, Polly?" Juicy Lucy asked. "You don't even like football."

"You heard what they said: the winning team gets a trophy."

"So?"

"So I LOVE trophies," Polly said. "I want it for myself." She glanced past the trees to the far side of the park where another football team was practising. "Hmm… and I think I know a way to get it."

Polly and Lucy ran across the park towards the other team. They were wearing gold-and-white-striped shirts. It was Hooray United, the team that Yuck's All Stars would be playing in the Cup Final.

"Coo-ee, I'm here," Polly called to them.

Hooray United's players looked over. "Who are you?" they asked.

Polly smiled. "I'm your new captain."

A tall boy with a chiseled jaw stepped forward. "You must have the wrong team. I'm the captain here."

"Not any more," Polly said, pushing the boy to the ground. She turned to the other players. "Hands up who wants to win that trophy next weekend?"

The players looked at one another, then raised their hands.

"Then do exactly as I say."

That afternoon, when Yuck arrived home, he saw Polly in her bedroom wearing a gold-and-white-striped football shirt. "Hey, where did you get that shirt?" he asked her.

Polly grinned. "I'm playing for Hooray United in the Cup Final."

Yuck looked puzzled. "Why would Hooray United want you on their team?"

"They made me captain," Polly replied smugly. "Now go away. Can't you see I'm busy? I'm making space for when I win that football trophy." Polly was standing by her chest of drawers where she kept her trophies: one for spelling and three for horse riding, plus two rosettes saying 1ST PLACE and the lucky horseshoe that she'd been given for her birthday from Pony Club. She moved the trophies apart, clearing space for one more.

"But you don't like playing football," Yuck said. "You don't even have have any football boots."

Polly smiled at her reflection in the shiny silver of her spelling trophy. "Mum says she's going to buy me a pair."

"Well, you'll still never win," Yuck told her.

Polly glared at him. "We'll see about that." And she pushed Yuck out of her room.

Yuck decided that when he was
EMPEROR OF EVERYTHING,
he'd captain the All Stars to the
World Cup Final. Instead of a
football they'd use Polly
wrapped in bouncy rubber
bands. Yuck would
dribble her up the
pitch, then POWER
STRIKE her
with his
lucky boots.
"Phwoargh!"
the crowd
would cheer
as she shot
upwards in
a stinky
cloud of gas,
right out of
the stadium.

For the next week, Yuck and his team went football crazy, excited about the big game ahead. For fun, at school, they tried out new yucky tactics. They coated their boots in slime and practised their sliding tackles.

They stuck chewing gum to their boots so they could run with the ball without it rolling away.

They made
a big green
bogey ball to
practise their
keepy-uppies,
kicking it up
and down
on a string
of snot.

They even played FARTBALL, blasting
the ball with their bottoms.

All week, Yuck's
lucky boots became
slimier and stickier
and snottier
and smellier.

Polly, on the other hand, didn't practise
at all. Instead she schemed with Lucy,
hatching a dastardly plan to win her
the trophy.

On the night before the big match, Yuck
put his lucky boots by his bed ready for the
morning. He lay down, smelling their pong
as he drifted off to sleep. He dreamed he
was the world's cheesiest POWER
STRIKER, blasting the ball at Hooray
United, knocking them down like skittles.

Meanwhile, Polly was awake, putting her dastardly plan into action. From her chest of drawers she picked up her lucky horseshoe and put it into her bag with her football kit. Then she tiptoed down the corridor to Yuck's bedroom door. She could hear him snoring in his bed, and through the keyhole she could smell the cheesy pong wafting from his lucky boots. She covered her nose and crept inside…

The next morning, Yuck woke up excited about the big match. But when he went to put his football kit on, his lucky boots had gone. "Hey, where are my football boots?" he said, running down the stairs.

"Yuck, your boots are here," Mum called from the kitchen.

Yuck rushed to fetch them, but to his surprise he saw Mum holding a cardboard box. She handed it to him. "I hope they fit," she said.

Yuck opened the box. Inside was a big pair of brand-new football boots.

"I bought Polly some boots and she insisted I get you some too," Mum said.

"She chose them herself," Dad said. "Wasn't that nice of her?"

"But these aren't my lucky boots," Yuck replied. They were huge and stiff and CLEAN!

"What's the matter?" Dad asked. "Don't you like them? Are they the wrong size?"

"Your old boots were mouldy and smelly, Yuck," Mum said. "These will look much smarter for the Cup Final."

At that moment, Polly stepped into the kitchen. "Go on, Yuck. Try them on," she sniggered.

"Polly, what have you done with my lucky boots?" Yuck asked.

Polly grinned. "I put them in the dustbin."

Yuck ran to the hallway and opened the front door. He saw a dustcart pulling away down the road. "No! Come back!" he called, running after it.

Yuck was too late. He stood in the street and watched as the dustcart disappeared around the corner.

"Unlucky, Yuck," Polly said from the doorway. "Your boots are going straight to the rubbish dump now."

Mum and Dad stepped to the car. "Well we'd better get going or you'll both be late for the match," Mum said.

Yuck didn't know what to do. All the way to the park, he stared out of the car window hoping to spot the dustcart so he could ask for his lucky boots back. But the dustcart was nowhere to be seen.

Polly sat beside him, singing:

"HOORAY FOR HOORAY UNiteD.
HOORAY, hOORAY FOR me.
HOORAY, hOORAY, hOORAY, hOORAY,
HOORAY, hOORAY, hOORee."

When they arrived at the park, Yuck saw
hundreds of people with scarves and
banners who'd come to watch.

There were stalls selling hot food and
drinks, and an ambulance
parked by the pitch with
two men in bright yellow
jackets unloading a
stretcher from its back.

"That's for you, Yuck," Polly sniggered.

"Good luck you two," Mum said.

"May the best team win," Dad added.

Yuck and Polly ran to the side of the pitch where both teams were warming up.

"What's the matter, Yuck? You look miserable," Little Eric said.

"I've got bad news," Yuck told him. "Polly threw away my lucky boots. Mum got me these ones instead."

He showed Little Eric his new boots.

"They're massive!" Litte Eric said.

"Polly chose them." They were much too big for Yuck, and they weren't comfortable at all. They weren't lucky and mouldy and they didn't stink of toe cheese.

Yuck glanced across at Hooray United warming up. Polly was pointing at him in his new boots, and her team were all laughing. "Good luck, clown feet," she called.

Over a loudspeaker, Yuck
heard an announcement:
"Two minutes until kick off."

Yuck called the All Stars into a huddle.
"Just do your best, everyone," he said,
trying not to show he was worried.

Both teams ran out onto the pitch and
the crowd of spectators began cheering.

"Welcome to the Cup Final," the
commentator announced over the
loudspeaker. "Hooray United versus the
All Stars."

The referee stood
in the centre circle
with Yuck and Polly.
He tossed a coin to
see which team
would kick off.

"Heads," Polly said.
"Tails," Yuck said.
Tails it was. The
whistle blew and Yuck
kicked the ball...

Yuck passed the ball across the pitch to
Kate the Skate who dribbled it up the
wing. As Hooray United tried to tackle
her, she crossed it to Tall Paul. Tall Paul
leapt up and headed it to Clip-Clop Chloe.
Clip-Clop Chloe ran towards the goal.

"That's it, Chloe! Shoot!" Yuck called.

But just as Clip-Clop Chloe was about to strike, Polly ran up behind her and booted her in the leg.

"Ouch!" Chloe cried, falling over.

The spectators booed and the referee blew his whistle. "Foul!"

Clip-Clop Chloe staggered to her feet. "That really hurt, Polly," she said, rubbing her leg. Then she looked at Polly's boot. Glued to its toe was a metal horseshoe.

"Hey, that's dangerous!" Clip-Clop Chloe said. "Referee, look at this!"

The referee ran over and saw the horseshoe on Polly's boot. He pulled a red card from his pocket and waved it at her. "Off!" he said.

"No way!" Polly replied. She snatched the card and tore it up, then booted the referee in the bottom.

"Ouch!" the referee said. He was so shocked that he swallowed his whistle. "**Tweet! Tweet! Tweet!**" he cried.

"Stretcher!" Polly called.

From the side of the pitch the two ambulance men in bright yellow jackets ran on and laid the referee on their stretcher. Polly sniggered as he was carried off injured.

An announcement came over the loudspeaker: "Ladies and Gentleman, the referee is injured so unfortunately the Cup Final cannot continue."

The crowd groaned with disappointment.

"It's OK. I'm here," a squeaky voice declared. From the crowd stepped a short man with glasses and a moustache. He had a pink top on and a whistle in his hand. "I'm a referee too. I'll take over," he said, skipping onto the pitch.

"Who's that?" Yuck whispered to Little Eric.

Little Eric scratched his head. "He looks kind of familiar."

The new referee picked the ball up and handed it to Polly. "Free kick to Hooray United," he said.

Polly grinned, putting the ball at her feet.

"But, ref, it was Polly who fouled," Yuck told him. "You need to send her off."

The new referee frowned at Yuck. "Don't argue with me," he said, and he winked at Polly.

Polly booted the ball towards the All Stars' end. "It's time to play dirty," she called.

Yuck watched in horror as Tom Bum ran for the ball and three of Hooray United's players charged after him, trampling him into the mud.

"Play on!" the referee called.

"But, referee, they're cheating!" Yuck said.

Yuck saw Hooray United's striker get the ball and shoot it towards the goal. Frank the Tank dived and caught it.

"Good save!" Yuck called.

The crowd cheered, but as they did, Hooray United's striker kicked the ball out of Frank the Tank's hands and into the back of the net.

"Hey, that's not allowed!" Frank the Tank said.

"GOAL!" the referee called. "One-nil!"

Hooray United celebrated, but the crowd booed.

Yuck ran to the referee. "Can't you see they're cheating?" he asked.

"No complaining or it'll be you who's sent off," the referee told him.

It was no use. Whenever the All Stars got the ball, Hooray United fouled them, and the referee paid no attention.

When Little Eric
made a run for
goal, two players
charged at him,
squeezing him in a
Hooray sandwich.

When Megan
the Mouth
dribbled the ball
up the pitch,
Hooray United
tripped her up and
she landed face
first in the mud.

When Frank the
Tank was defending
a free kick, Hooray
United tied his laces
to the goalpost so
he couldn't dive.
The ball shot
straight past him.
"GOAL! Two-nil!"

"I can't believe they're two goals ahead," Yuck said to Little Eric as they went back to the centre circle to kick off again.

"We've got to do something, Yuck," Little Eric replied.

But Yuck could hardly run in his new boots. They were far too big for him. If only I had my lucky boots, he thought, then I'd show these cheats a thing or two. But his lucky boots would be miles away on the rubbish dump by now.

At that moment, Yuck had an idea. "Little Eric, I'm going to need you to be captain for a while," he said.

"Me?" Little Eric asked. "Why?"

Yuck winked then stepped to the centre circle. He kicked off, tapping the ball into the air, first with his right foot then with his left, doing keepie-uppies. Polly tried to get it from him but she couldn't.

"What are you going to do, Polly?" Yuck
asked. "Cheat and stamp on my foot?"

"Good idea," Polly said, and
she stamped down hard on
the toe of Yuck's new boot.

"Ouch!" Yuck said, falling to the ground.

"Oh, sorry, did I hurt you?" Polly giggled.

"Stretcher!" Yuck called.

Little Eric ran to Yuck's side. "Are you
OK, Yuck? What's Polly done to you?"

Yuck was writhing on the ground. "Oh,
my foot! My foot hurts! I need to go off."

From the side of the pitch, the ambulance
men ran on with their stretcher. They lifted
Yuck onto it.

Polly sniggered as they carried him
away. "Good riddance," she said.

"What are we going to do now?" Megan the Mouth said, shocked.

"We'll never win without Yuck," Clip-Clop Chloe said.

But while Yuck was being carried off, he whispered in Little Eric's ear. "It's OK, I just have to go somewhere. While I'm gone I  want you to try some new tactics."

Yuck whispered the new tactics to Little Eric, and Little Eric smiled.

As the All Stars watched Yuck being carried off, the referee blew his whistle and Polly booted the ball up the field. The All Stars were caught off-guard. Frank the Tank was still looking at Yuck when the ball rolled straight past him.

"GOAL!" the referee called.

"Hey, we weren't ready!" Tom Bum said.

The referee blew his whistle again. "Half-time! That's three-nil to Hooray United!"

Yuck was being lifted off the stretcher into the back of the ambulance. Sitting next to him was the injured referee.

"Hello," Yuck said to him. "Are you OK?"

"Tweet," the referee replied, his whistle still stuck in his throat.

"That girl who kicked you is my sister," Yuck told him. "She's cheating. We have to stop her."

"You're not doing anything until we've checked your toes, young man," one of the ambulance men said to Yuck. "They might be broken."

Yuck took off his boots and his socks and smiled at the ambulance men. "It's OK, my toes are fine," he said, wiggling them. "These boots are much too big for me. My toes don't reach the end."

The ambulance men looked at one another, puzzled. "You mean you're not injured?"

"No," Yuck replied. "I came off because I need your help. Could you drive me to the rubbish dump, please?"

"The rubbish dump? What for?"

"There's no time to explain," Yuck said. He turned to the referee. "It's the only way we can stop Polly."

The referee gestured for the ambulance men to hurry. "Tweet! Tweet!" he said.

"Right you are," they replied. They jumped in and turned on the siren.

As the ambulance sped away with its siren wailing, Little Eric gathered the All Stars into a huddle and told them the new tactics.

Quickly, they prepared: Fartin Martin ran to a stall selling hot food and ordered a baked potato with a triple helping of baked beans; Tom Bum ordered a hotdog; Ben Bong searched for worms; Schoolie Julie fetched slime from the pond. Then they took up their positions, ready for the second half. In the centre circle, Little Eric faced Polly.

"Ready to lose, are you?" Polly asked.

"We're not giving up without a fight," Little Eric told her.

The referee blew his whistle and the All Stars put their new tactics into play…

Fartin Martin scoffed his triple helping of baked beans. When three Hooray United players ran to tackle him, he bent over and let a ripper fire from his shorts. The players flew backwards into the mud.

"What a honker!" the crowd cheered.

Tom Bum slid his hotdog into the pocket of Hooray United's winger. Its smell wafted

across the pitch and a dog ran from the crowd and chased the boy across the park, yapping at his shorts.

"Woof! Woof!"

Kate the Skate slimed her boots. When Hooray United's striker got the ball, she skidded across the pitch doing the most amazing sliding tackle.

Ben Bong had a handful of worms. When one of Hooray United's midfielders tried to tackle him, Ben Bong slipped the worms into the boy's shorts. They wriggled where they shouldn't, and the crowd looked in horror as the boy yanked his shorts to his ankles trying to pull the worms out.

Meanwhile, Yuck was speeding across town in the ambulance. It sped down a winding road to the town's rubbish dump. To Yuck's surprise there were other ambulances there and a fire engine and a police car too. The ambulance skidded to a halt and Yuck jumped out. "Thanks!" he said to the driver.

In front of Yuck was a huge hill of rubbish. Men wearing radiation suits and gas masks were climbing over it.

A policemen stepped to Yuck's side. "I'd stay away from here if I were you," the policeman said. "Someone's dumped some toxic waste. Very dangerous toxic waste."

"But I have to find my lucky boots," Yuck said, and he raced up the rubbish pile.

"Wait! Come back!" the policeman called. "It's too dangerous!"

Yuck began searching for his boots.

There was all sorts of rubbish on the town dump: old vegetables… stinky underpants… mouldy pizza… dirty nappies… cold spaghetti… snotty tissues… rotting compost. It smelt revolting.

"I've found the toxic waste!" a man called out. At the top of the mound Yuck saw a man in a radiation suit holding up a pair of football boots.

Yuck rushed to him. "Those are my lucky boots," he said. They'd been stewing on the rubbish dump all morning. They were even mouldier and smellier than before.

"These are the most revolting football boots I've ever encountered," the man said, sealing them in a plastic bag. "They're too disgusting even for the rubbish dump."

"But I need them," Yuck told him. "They're my lucky boots. I'm the captain of the All Stars, and I'm supposed to be playing in the Cup Final."

"The Cup Final? But hasn't that already started?" the man replied.

"Yes, this is an emergency."

The man handed Yuck his lucky boots. "In that case you'd better hurry. Though I wouldn't wear them without cleaning them first. They're highly contaminated."

"Thank you," Yuck said, and he raced down the heap of rubbish and leapt back into the ambulance. "Full speed ahead," he said.

Back at the game, the All Stars were continuing with their new tactics.

Frank the Tank had been picking his nose making a big bouncy bogey ball. He booted it up the pitch, and when one of Hooray United's midfielders tried to head it, bogeys splattered all over him.

Tall Paul used mud and twigs to style his

hair into a nest. So, instead of heading the ball, he caught it in his hair, high up where Hooray United couldn't reach it.

Megan the Mouth and Clip-Clop Chloe
tied their shoelaces to one another's boots.

When Hooray
United's striker
ran towards
them, they
stepped apart
and the laces
pulled tight,
sending him
flying.

Schoolie Julie tied one end of a piece of
elastic to Hooray United's goalpost and the
other to their defender's ankle. When the
defender tried to run upfield he went
pinging back into the goal.

While the other All Stars were keeping the Hooray United players busy, Little Eric pulled his shirt above his head and balanced the football on top. He put his glasses on the ball to disguise it, then ran all the way up the pitch, stepping straight past Hooray United's goalkeeper. He pulled down his shirt and the football rolled off his head into the net. "Tricked you!" he said.

The referee blew his whistle. "Errr, GOAL," he called. "I think."

"What an incredible move!" the commentator announced over the loudspeaker. "The All Stars have got a goal back! That's three-one to Hooray United. With only a minute to go!"

"Come on, team, we can do it," Little Eric called.

"A minute to go? You'll never win!" Polly sneered.

At that moment, from across the park came the sound of an ambulance siren. The ambulance screeched to a halt and Yuck jumped out wearing his lucky boots.

"Phwoargh!" the crowd cried. "What's that smell?"

"What's this? The All Stars' star player is back!" the commentator announced.

"Pass me the ball!" Yuck called, running onto the pitch. Little Eric crossed the ball and Yuck began dribbling it, winding between Hooray United's players. With each kick, a revolting smell puffed up from his lucky boots: old vegetables… stinky underpants… mouldy pizza… dirty nappies… cold spaghetti… snotty tissues… rotting compost.

Hooray United's players backed away coughing and spluttering. One by one they fainted and fell over.

"Stop him, you wimps!" Polly shouted.

But Yuck's lucky boots were too powerful. He approached the goal and struck the ball hard. A cheesy cloud engulfed the goalkeeper and the ball flew into the back of the net.

"GOAL!" the crowd cheered.

the loudspeaker announced.
are only ten seconds to go!"
ran to the centre circle to kick off
gain. Hooray United's players were all
lying on the ground, coughing. Only Polly
was still on her feet. She sprinted to her
goal. "You'll never get it past me," she cried.

Yuck took a run up. From the
half-way line he struck the ball
at FULL POWER.

An explosion of cheesy gas
launched from his boot
and the ball rocketed
towards Polly.

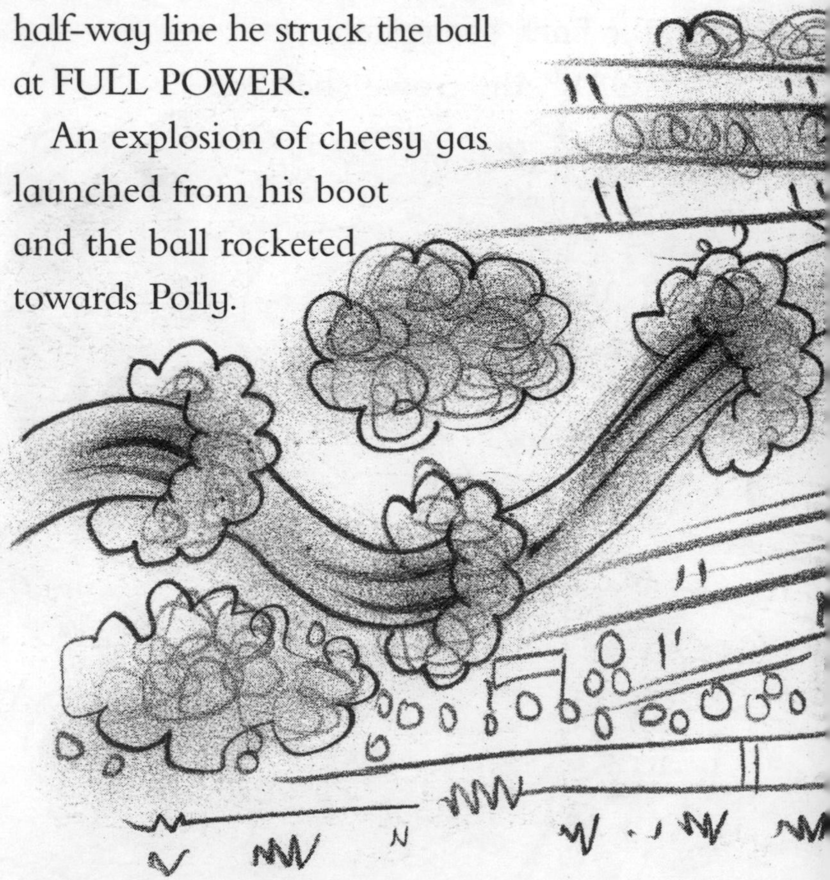

It was the greatest POWER STRIKE
EVER. The ball dipped and swerved in a
storm of stinky toe cheese. It knocked Polly
clear off her feet, into the back of the goal.

"GOAL!" the referee called. He blew his
whistle for full time and the crowd cheered.

"What a fantastic football match!" Yuck heard over the loudspeaker. "Three goals each! It's a draw!"

Polly hung tangled in the net, coughing and spluttering. She screamed at the referee. "I'm supposed to win, you idiot! Why didn't you stop the match earlier?" She untangled herself then marched over and kicked the referee in the shin.

"Ouch! Polly, that hurt," the referee cried. "I thought we were friends."

"Hang on a second. That's not a referee," Yuck said. He grabbed hold of the referee's moustache and it came off in his hand.

"Ouch!" the referee squeaked. It was Juicy Lucy in disguise! The real referee came running back onto the pitch.

"Tweet!" he called. He had a red card in his hand.

"What did you say, ref?" Yuck asked him. Yuck gave the real referee a pat on the back and the whistle shot out from his throat.

The referee waved the red card at Lucy. "I said, 'OFF'!" he said to her.

Lucy ashamedly picked up her moustache and hobbled off the pitch.

The referee turned to Polly. "As for you, you're in BIG TROUBLE." He bent down and yanked Polly's boot off then held it in the air for the crowd to see. "This girl is a cheat," he announced. "She has a horseshoe stuck to her boot."

The crowd gasped when they saw it.

"Polly, what a terrible thing to do!" Mum called from the crowd.

"I've never been so ashamed in all my life," Dad called.

"Hooray United are hereby disqualified," the referee announced. "I declare Yuck's All Stars the winners!"

The crowd cheered: "All Stars! All Stars! All Stars!"

Hooray United's players scowled at Polly. "You silly girl. Your cheating made us lose."

Mum and Dad came on to the pitch and dragged Polly away in shame.

The referee presented the trophy to Yuck and the All Stars. "Well done to all of you," he said, pinching his nose as the pong wafted up from Yuck's boots.

Yuck glanced across the pitch at Polly being bundled into the car. He smiled then, in a cloud of cheesy gas, lifted the trophy above his head. "Three cheers for the All Stars!"

YUCK'S CREEPY CRAWLIES

Yuck was in the garden playing with his creepy crawly castle. He'd built it out of mud. It had a flag on its top and a caterpillar was crawling up the flagpole. Ants and earwigs were scurrying on its towers and turrets. Beetles and centipedes were scuttling over its walls. Worms and slugs were peering from its windows, and guarding the castle's entrance was an enormous hairy spider.

Yuck was King of the castle, and the creepy crawlies were his brave knights. They were defending the castle against the Pink Attackers, two plastic dolls that belonged to Yuck's sister, Polly Princess.

"Here come the enemy," Yuck said, placing the dolls on the castle's walls as though they were trying to climb in.

"Knights to the rescue!"

Yuck watched as the creepy crawlies
began crawling onto the dolls. Ants and
beetles scurried over their dresses and hair.
Worms and caterpillars wrapped around
their arms and legs. "That's it, take them
prisoner!" Yuck said. "No one invades
creepy crawly castle and lives."

Polly Princess called from the back door. "Yuck, have you seen my dolls anywhere?"

"What dolls?" Yuck called back.

Polly saw the dolls on his muddy castle. "Hey, what have you done to them?" she yelled, running over.

"But they were attacking creepy crawly castle," Yuck explained.

Polly grabbed the dolls. "Urgh!" she screamed. "They're covered in creepy crawlies!" She shook them furiously, sending ants, beetles and worms flying in all directions.

"Hey, be careful!" Yuck told her. He searched the grass, checking his creepy crawlies were OK.

Polly kicked his castle, knocking over a tower. "I HATE creepy crawlies!" she said, and she ran back into the house.

A moment later, the back door opened again and Mum leaned out. "Yuck, come indoors at once," she called.

"But, Mum—"

"Now, Yuck! You're not allowed to play outside anymore."

Yuck saw Polly at the window sticking her tongue out. Trust her to ruin everything, he thought.

"I'll be just a second," Yuck called. Quickly, he began gathering his creepy crawlies, slipping them into his pockets. "It's time to move location," he whispered to them, heading indoors.

"Look at the state of you," Mum said as Yuck stepped into the kitchen. "Take those muddy shoes off at once." Mum fetched a cloth and wiped his muddy hands.

Yuck eyed Polly at the sink cleaning her dolls with soapy water. There were more dolls on the kitchen table, all with neatly brushed hair and rosy cheeks. Polly had given them a beauty makeover that morning.

"Yuck, why can't you play nicely like your sister?" Mum asked him.

"Because he's revolting, Mum," Polly interrupted, flicking water at Yuck.

Yuck picked a lump of mud from his knee and threw it back. It splatted Polly's ear.

"Urgh!" Polly yelled.

"Stop that, both of you!" Mum said. "For the rest of the day I want the two of you to play indoors where I can keep an eye on you. And I want you to play nicely together."

"Together?" Polly asked, shocked.

"With Polly?" Yuck asked.

"Yes," Mum told them. "And I don't want any fighting."

"But Mum, it's no fun playing with Polly. She cheats and she never let's me play what I want," Yuck said.

"How about we play hide-and-seek?" Polly said.

"Oh, do we have to?" Yuck sighed.

Mum frowned at Yuck. "Yes, Yuck," she said. "I told you: you're to play nicely together."

"But Polly always hides in the toilet and locks the door so I can't get in to find her."

"No hiding in the toilet, Polly," Mum said.

Polly fluttered her eyelashes. "OK, Mum," she replied sweetly. "Now close your eyes, Yuck, and count to ten." Polly ran out of the kitchen.

Yuck closed his eyes and started counting. "One… two… three…"

He could feel the creepy crawlies wriggling in his pockets. He wanted to play with them. "…four… five… six… seven…"

Didn't Mum and Polly realise that the King of creepy crawly castle had better

things to do than play hide-and-seek? he
thought. "…eight… nine… ten!"

Yuck opened his eyes and raced from the
kitchen. He ran straight to the downstairs
toilet and tried turning the door handle,
but the door was locked. He could hear
giggling coming from inside. "I know
you're in there, Polly," he said.

The giggling stopped. Polly was
pretending that she wasn't there.

Yuck heard a click and saw the light go
out under the door. "Oh, Polly, don't cheat."

But still there was no reply.

Yuck glanced to the stairs. He had an idea. "Oh, well," he said loudly. "I guess Polly must be somewhere else. I'll have to go and search for her."

Yuck ran straight upstairs to his room. If Polly wanted to cheat then he might as well let her, he thought. Hiding in the toilet, she wouldn't know whether he was looking for her or not.

Yuck took the creepy crawlies from his pockets and placed them on his bedroom carpet. "OK, knights. It's time to play!"

Yuck went to his wardrobe and fetched
a carrier bag of bogeys that he'd been
collecting, then he set to work on a new
creepy crawly castle.
He piled handfuls
of bogeys, one on
top of the other,
building green
walls, towers
and turrets.

He used a pencil
for a flagpole and
tied a smelly sock
to it as a flag.

Then he poured
a pot of GO GLOW
SLIME in a ring
around the castle,
making a
slimy moat.

The creepy crawlies crawled onto their new home. The caterpillars climbed up the flagpole. The ants and woodlice scurried onto the bogey towers. The beetles and earwigs scuttled over the bogey walls. The centipedes, slugs and worms wiggled in the windows, and the big fat spider sat guard at the entrance.

When his knights were in position, Yuck crept into Polly's room and borrowed another one of her dolls. He stood it on the castle. "Quickly, knights, the enemy's attacking," he said.

The creepy crawlies scurried onto the doll, wriggling, crawling and nipping. The doll slid down the bogey walls into the slimy moat and the big fat spider began spinning it in a web. "That's it, knights! Show the prisoner no mercy!"

Yuck decided that when he was EMPEROR OF EVERYTHING, he would live in a great big creepy crawly castle. His creepy crawly knights would wear suits of armour, and if Polly tried to attack the castle, she'd be captured and locked in the dungeon with the ghosts.

Meanwhile, Polly was still hiding in the toilet, thinking how clever she was that Yuck would be searching everywhere for her. A whole hour passed until she finally came out. "I'm the winner!" she called.

There was no reply.

She went looking for Yuck and found him playing in his bedroom. "Hey, you're meant to be looking for me!" she said.

"But you cheated," Yuck told her, adjusting the flag on his castle.

Polly saw her doll lying in the slimy moat, wrapped in a spider's web and writhing with creepy crawlies. "Hey, give that back!" she said, grabbing it. She shook it, showering creepy crawlies all over Yuck's room. "I hate you, Yuck! I'm telling Mum!"

Polly ran out and thumped down the stairs. "Mum, Yuck's got creepy crawlies in the house!"

Quickly, Yuck gathered up the creepy crawlies, put them back on the castle and hid it under his bed.

Yuck fetched a bag of scabs from his wardrobe and emptied them onto the floor. He pretended he was playing tiddly winks, using a big knee-scab to flick smaller elbow-scabs into a mouldy old mug.

His door opened and Polly came in with Mum.

"Yuck, have you been playing with creepy crawlies in here?" Mum asked.

"No, Mum, I've been playing tiddlywinks," Yuck replied.

"No, he hasn—" But as Polly spoke,
three scabs flicked across the room into her
mouth. "Urgh!"

Mum was looking around for signs of creepy crawlies, but couldn't see any. "Yuck, you're supposed to be playing hide-and-seek with Polly," she said.

"But Polly cheated," Yuck explained. "She locked herself in the toilet again."

Mum looked at Polly crossly. "Is that true?" she asked.

But Polly could barely speak. "Bwa…" She was picking chewy bits of scab from her teeth.

"Well if you two can't play hide-and-seek nicely together, then we'll have to find something else for you to play," Mum said.

"It's OK, Mum. I'm happy playing on my own," Yuck told her.

"Oh, no you don't, Yuck," Mum said. "I want you both to come downstairs with me. How about you play a board game together?"

Mum headed out with Polly following.

"Can we play *MILLIONAIRE MAKER*, Mum?" Polly asked.

"Of course you can. That'll be fun," Mum said.

Yuck reached under his bed and grabbed a handful of creepy crawlies. "Come on. Come and play too," he whispered, sneaking them into his pocket.

Polly set up the board game in the living room. *MILLIONAIRE MAKER* was Polly's favourite board game. The aim was to move around the board collecting gold coins as you went. Whoever got the most gold coins was the winner.

"I'll be the pink car and you can be the paperclip," Polly said. Yuck always had to be the paperclip. It should have been a blue car, but that piece was lost.

"I'll go first," Polly said. She rolled a five, then moved her pink car around the board. Yuck counted her moving eight squares, not five, so she landed on a gold coin. "Oh, look, lucky me," she said.

"But you cheated. I saw," Yuck said.

"No I didn't," Polly replied, taking the gold coin and placing it by her side.

Yuck took his turn. He rolled the dice and Polly stopped it with her knee.

"One," she said. "Unlucky."

Yuck moved his paper clip one square, then Polly took another turn. This time,

Yuck counted her moving her car thirteen squares to another gold coin. "You're cheating again," he said.

In no time at all Polly had a pile of gold coins by her side and Yuck had none.

Yuck had an idea. He sneaked a handful of ants from his pocket and placed them on the carpet.

Polly rolled the dice and moved her piece. "Oh, look! I'm the winner!" she said, taking the last gold coin from the board.

"No you're not," Yuck replied, smiling. By his side was now a pile of gold coins.

"Hey, how did you get those?" Polly asked. She looked – her pile of coins had vanished. Then behind her she saw coins rolling across the carpet. "What's going on?" she asked, picking one up. "Urgh! Ants!" Polly cried. Ants were rolling Polly's coins to Yuck.

She leapt to her feet. "I'm telling Mum!"

As Polly ran off, Yuck gathered the ants and slipped them back into his pocket.

 Mum came running in. "Where are they, Yuck?" she asked. "Polly says you've brought ants in here."

Yuck shrugged his shoulders and looked around. "I don't know what she's talking about, Mum," he said.

Mum looked at Polly, puzzled.

"He did!" Polly said. "They were in here a minute ago!"

"Polly's just angry because I won," Yuck said, showing Mum his pile of gold coins.

Mum tutted at Polly. "Oh, do play nicely, Polly," she said, and she fetched another game from the shelf. "Here you are, you can play *SNAKES AND LADDERS* instead."

Polly snatched the box moodily and began laying the game on the floor. "You wait, Yuck. I'm going to thrash you now."

"And no fighting," Mum told them, leaving the room.

In *SNAKES AND LADDERS* you had to
get from the bottom of the board to the
top. If you landed on a ladder you could
go up, but if you landed on a snake you
had to slide back down.

"I'm going first," Polly said, snatching the
dice. She rolled a four, but Yuck saw her
move her counter eight squares so she landed
on a ladder. She climbed up three rows.
"Ha! I'm already beating you," she said.

Yuck pretended he hadn't noticed her
cheating. Instead, he had a plan...

Yuck waited until Polly had almost
reached the top of the board, then dipped
his hand into his pocket, pulling out a long
wriggly worm. As Polly shook the dice, he

sneaked the worm onto the
board, laying it from top to
bottom. "Oh, what a shame,"
he said. "Look, Polly, you're
on a snake. You've got to slide
all the way down."

Polly stared, confused. "How did that get
there? I wasn't on a snake before," she said.

Then the snake wiggled.

"Watch out!
It's going to bite!"
Yuck said.

Polly shrieked
and leapt to her feet.

"Hang on. That's
not a snake, that's
a worm!" she
yelled. "Right, I'm
not playing with
you anymore! I'm
telling Mum!"

Polly ran out of
the room in a huff.

Yuck picked up the worm and smiled.
"Good work," he said to it. "Now we get to
play without her."

Yuck ran out through the door, heading for his room. As he passed the kitchen he heard Polly complaining to Mum. "I'm not playing with Yuck anymore," she said. "He's disgusting. He put a worm on the board!"

Yuck raced to his bedroom and reached under his bed for his creepy crawly castle. But just as he was about to pull it out, he heard footsteps coming up the stairs. He quickly scooped lumps of bogey from a turret, then rolled them into balls pretending he was playing marbles. The door opened and Polly came back in with Mum.

"Yuck, what's all this about you playing with a worm?" Mum asked.

Yuck looked up. "I don't know what you're talking about. I've been playing marbles," he said.

"He HAS got a worm, Mum!" Polly said. "And lots of other creepy crawlies too. They're in here somewh—" As Polly spoke, two big bogeys shot into her mouth. "Urgh!"

Mum looked around the room. "Polly, there aren't any creepy crawlies in here. I don't know what's got into you today."

But Polly could barely speak. "Bwu…" She was pulling sticky bogeys from her teeth.

"There must be something you two can play nicely together." Mum said. "What about a computer game?"

"Bagsy we play *WONDERLAND*," Polly said, following Mum out.

Yuck took another handful of creepy crawlies. He ran after them. "*WONDERLAND* is too easy. Can't we play *ALIEN INVADER*?"

But Polly was already at the computer holding one of the controls. "I was here first, and we're playing *WONDERLAND*."

"And no fighting," Mum said, heading downstairs.

WONDERLAND was set in an enchanted forest and the aim of the game was to fly a fairy through the trees collecting magic stars.

Yuck groaned as Polly started the game and selected her fairy character. She chose to be Buttercup. "Buttercup's the best fairy," she said, clicking her controller, flying Buttercup between rainbow-coloured trees.

Yuck picked up the other controller, then took a centipede from his pocket and placed it beside the computer terminal. He watched as it crawled through a hole in the side of the computer.

"Look, there's a magic star," Polly said, landing Buttercup on a branch. But as the fairy was about to pick the star up, an enormous centipede wriggled along the branch behind her.

"What on earth's that?" Polly said, staring at it.

Yuck giggled. His centipede was inside the computer game. It was HUGE! He pressed his controller and it opened its jaws, then started eating Polly's fairy.

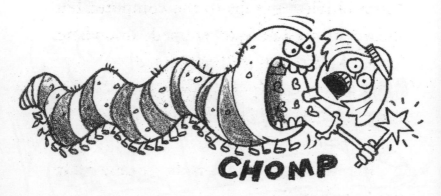

CHOMP

"Hey, it's gobbling Buttercup!" Polly shrieked. "What's going on?"

She saw Yuck giggling. "Hey! Are you doing that?"

Yuck pressed eject on the game, and his centipede crawled out from a slot in the front of the computer.

"It WAS you!" Polly cried, seeing the centipede. "I'm telling Mum!"

As Polly stormed down the stairs, Yuck picked up the centipede and slipped it into his pocket. Then he loaded *ALIEN INVADER* and began blasting aliens across the screen.

He heard Mum coming out of the kitchen. "Polly, you'd better not be lying," she said. Mum hurried upstairs to the computer, but there was no sign of a centipede anywhere.

"Yuck, where is it?" Polly asked.

Yuck shrugged his shoulders. "I don't know what she's talking about, Mum," he said.

Mum frowned at Polly.

"But, Mum, he put it in the computer. It ate Buttercup!"

"Polly, what's the matter with you today?" Mum asked.

"She's just angry because she's no good at *ALIEN INVADER*," Yuck said.

Mum pulled the plug on the computer. "Right, you two, I've had enough of this!"

"Oh, Mum, I was about to save the universe!"

"You're supposed to be playing nicely together," Mum reminded them. "There must something you can play without arguing.'

That afternoon, Yuck and Polly tried playing all sorts of things together. They tried doing some colouring-in, but Polly refused to share the crayons. As she was colouring a picture of a flower, Yuck took a caterpillar from his pocket and swapped it with the green crayon. When Polly tried to colour the flower's leaves, the caterpillar nibbled them.

"Stop!" Polly cried, seeing it munching through her piece of paper. Soon, where her flower should have been was just a great big hole.

They tried singing karaoke together, but Polly wouldn't share the microphone. As she was changing songs on the karaoke machine, Yuck swapped the microphone with a big fat slug.

"Urgh!" Polly said as she was about to sing. She was holding the slug to her mouth.

They tried dressing up together, but Polly insisted on choosing the costumes. She wore a princess's dress and made Yuck wear one too. As she was styling her hair, he swapped her hairgrip with a beetle, and it began cutting Polly's fringe with its claws.

"Eek!" she screamed, looking in the mirror.

They even tried a staring contest, but Polly cheated yet again, holding her eyes open with her fingers. As she stared, Yuck took an earwig from his pocket and slipped it onto her lap. It crawled up her arm, then into her ear. Yuck giggled, seeing the earwig crawl right through from one ear to the other.

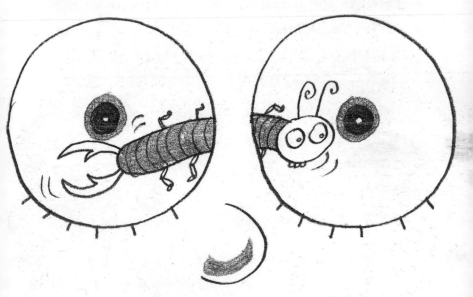

"Aaarrrrgh!" Polly screamed, shaking her head.

"I win!" Yuck said.

"Get it out! Get it out!"

The earwig fell from Polly's ear onto the carpet, and she ran to find Mum. "Mum, Yuck's at it again!"

Yuck slipped the earwig into his pocket then ran after her. "No I'm not, Mum," he said, stepping into the kitchen.

Mum looked crossly at the two of them. "What's the matter now?" she asked.

"It's Yuck's creepy crawlies," Polly replied. "He's been getting me with them all day. He put ants on *MILLIONAIRE MAKER*, a worm on *SNAKES AND LADDERS,* and a centipede in *WONDERLAND.* He swapped my crayon with a caterpillar, my hairgrip with a beetle and my microphone with a slug. And now an earwig just crawled into my ear!"

"Is this true, Yuck?" Mum asked.

Yuck shrugged his shoulders. "I've no idea what she's talking about, Mum," he said innocently.

Polly was fuming with anger. "You liar, Yuck! I know you've got creepy crawlies. I saw you playing with them this morning when you were meant to be playing hide-and-seek with me."

"But you cheated at hide-and-seek," Yuck reminded her. "You locked yourself in the toilet."

"Stop arguing!" Mum told them.

Polly scowled at Yuck, and Yuck scowled back.

"Why can't you two play nicely together?" Mum asked.

"OK, let's have another go at hide-and-seek," Polly said. "I bet I beat you again, Yuck!"

Mum looked at Polly. "Do you promise not to hide in the toilet?" she asked.

"I promise," Polly replied. "Now close your eyes, Yuck, and count to ten."

Yuck closed his eyes and Polly ran out of the kitchen. "One… two… three…"

Yuck knew there was no way Polly wouldn't hide in the toilet. She always cheated and locked the door. "…four… five… six… seven…" Yuck had a plan: a plan to make sure that Polly would never cheat again. "…eight… nine… ten."

He opened his eyes, then ran to find her. He raced straight to the toilet door and tried the handle. Just as he'd suspected, it was locked. He listened and heard Polly giggling inside. She'd done it again. "Oh, I wonder where Polly could be?" he said loudly.

The giggling stopped, and through the gap under the door he saw the toilet light go out. It's time for her to pay, he thought. My knights will deal with this.

Yuck ran to his room and took his creepy crawly castle out from under his bed. "Knights, it's time for battle," he said. "The enemy's not far away. We must ambush them while they least expect it."

Yuck assembled the creepy crawlies into
platoons: the ants, the caterpillars, the slugs,
the beetles, the worms, the centipedes and
the earwigs. At their head he placed the big
fat spider. "Follow me," he whispered. "It's
going to be a surprise attack."

Yuck led his creepy crawlies down the stairs to the toilet door, then whispered his commands.

The centipedes and earwigs scurried under the door, heading in first. Then the earwigs and slugs followed, then the beetles, caterpillars, ants and worms. Lastly, the big fat spider squeezed under the door.

Inside the toilet, Polly was hiding in the dark. She could hear the scurrying of tiny feet. All of a sudden she felt something crawling up her leg. She brushed it off, but then something else crawled up her arm.

"Eek!" she cried, feeling for the light switch. Her hand touched the wall. "Urgh! What's going on?" The wall felt as if it was alive and wriggling. Polly turned the light on...

The creepy crawlies dived from the walls, leapt from the sink and hurled themselves from the toilet, attacking Polly. Earwigs poured into her ears and beetles swarmed over her hair. Ants scurried across her face

and caterpillars scuttled up her nose. Slugs
slimed her neck, centipedes crawled down
her T-shirt and worms wriggled in her
pants. "AAARRRGGGHHH!" Polly
screamed. "HELP!"

"I've found you, Polly," Yuck called from outside the toilet door. He was laughing.

"Get them off me!" he heard Polly crying.

Mum came running to Yuck. "What's happened?" she asked.

"I've found Polly," Yuck told her. "She's locked herself in the toilet again."

"Locked herself in the toilet?"

"I'm afraid so," Yuck said. "She's been cheating again."

"Help!" Polly cried.

"Polly, what are you doing in there?" Mum asked. "I told you not to hide in the toilet." Mum tried to open the toilet door, but it was locked. "Polly, come out at once," she called.

But Polly couldn't get out. Guarding the
door handle was a big fat spider.

"I hate you, Yuck!" she screamed.

Mum banged on the door. "Come out
this instant, Polly! Stop messing about!"

Yuck was laughing. "Oh, well, Mum, if
Polly's stuck then I guess I'm going to have
to play on my own after all."

With that, Yuck ran off up the stairs. At
the top he stopped and called down.
"Knights regroup!"

While Mum was trying to open the
door, on the ground by her feet creepy
crawlies were sneaking from the toilet, one
by one, and scurrying up the stairs.

"Well done, knights," Yuck said to them.
"Victory is ours!"